Pignic

Anne Miranda
Illustrations by Rosekrans Hoffman

BOYDS MILLS PRESS

To Saturnino with salsa!—A.M.

For Eileen —R.H.

Published by Caroline House
Boyds Mills Press, Inc.
A Highlights Company
815 Church Street
Honesdale, Pennsylvania 18431
Printed in Mexico

Publisher Cataloging-in-Publication Data
Miranda, Anne.
Pignic ; an alphabet book in rhyme / by Anne Miranda ; illustrated by Rosekrans Hoffman.—1st ed.
[32]p. : col. ill. ; cm.
Summary : Pigs gather for their annual picnic in this rhyming alphabet book.
ISBN 1-56397-558-0
1. Children's poetry, American. 2. Alphabet rhymes—Juvenile poetry.
3. Alphabet—Juvenile poetry. [1. American poetry. 2. Alphabet rhymes—Poetry. 3. Alphabet.] I. Hoffman, Rosekrans, ill. II. Title.
808.81—dc20 1996 AC
Library of Congress Catalog Card Number 95-78287

First edition, 1996
Book designed by Kirchoff/Wohlberg, Inc.
The text of this book is set in 30-point Goudy.
The illustrations are done in pencil and colored inks.
Distributed by St. Martin's Press

10 9 8 7 6 5 4 3 2 1

The annual family pignic
came only once a year.

With picnic baskets on their arms,
pigs came from far and near.

Aa

Auntie Anne made apple pie.

Bb

Ben brought beans from Boston.

Cc

Cousin Cabe baked carrot cake.

Dd

Some dates arrived with Dustin.

Ee

Evan cooked eel and eggplant stew.

Ff

Fern fried fifty fish.

Gg

Gram made cold gazpacho soup.

Hh

Hank had a hominy dish.

Ii

Ivan churned the ice cream.

Jj

June brought jam in jars.

Kk

Karl made pickled kumquat mousse,

Ll

and the lemon tarts were Lars'.

Mm

May made mush and meatballs.

Nn

Niles brought nectarines.

Oo

Ollie stirred the onion sauce.

Pp

Paul picked peas and greens.

Qq

Grampa Quigly sliced some quince.

Rr

Ray steamed pots of rice.

Ss

Sister Seti strained spaghetti.

Tt

Tyler's tea was iced.

Uu

Una brought some ugly fruit.

Vv

Violet brought vermicelli.

Ww

Walt carved watermelon boats.

Xx

Max took extra jelly.

Yy

Yolanda mashed some yellow yams.

Zz

Zak baked zucchini bread.

"It's the finest pignic ever!"

That's what everybody said.

Aa  apple pie

Bb 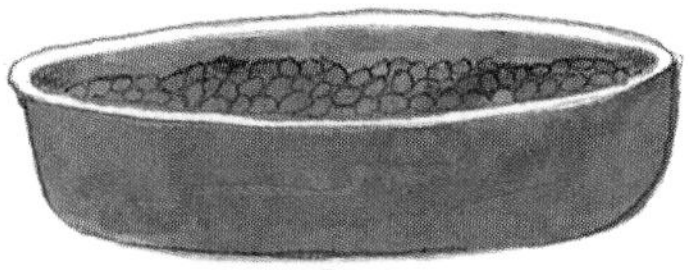 beans

Cc  carrot cake

Dd 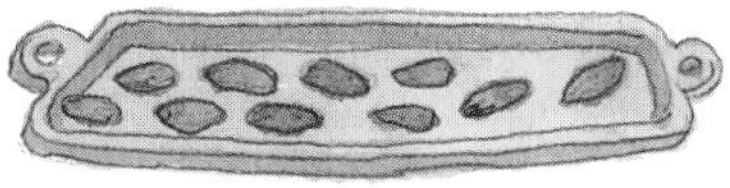 dates

Ee  eggplant stew

Ff 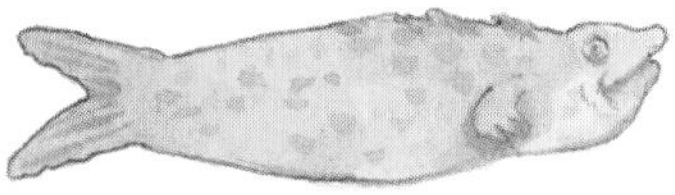 fish

Gg  gazpacho soup

Hh 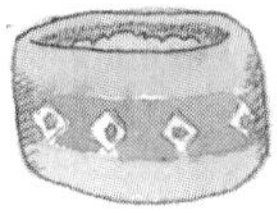 hominy dish

Ii 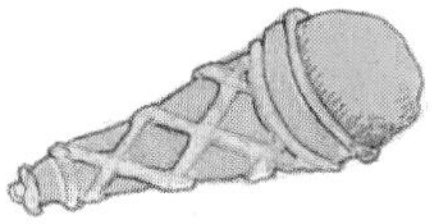 ice cream

Jj  jam

Kk  kumquat mousse

Ll  lemon tarts

Mm 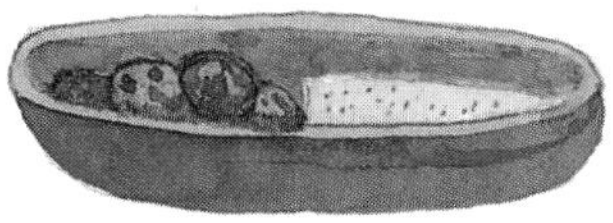 meatballs

Nn  nectarines

Oo  onion sauce

Pp  peas

Qq 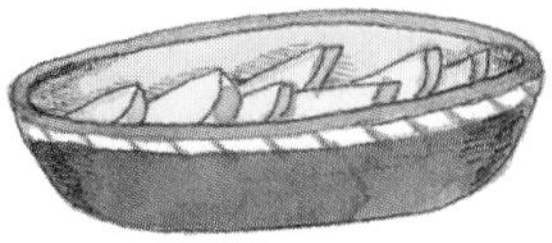 quince

Rr  rice

Ss 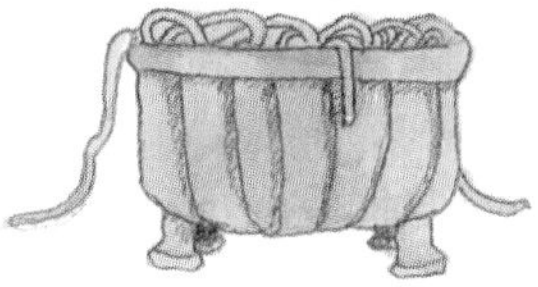 spaghetti

Tt 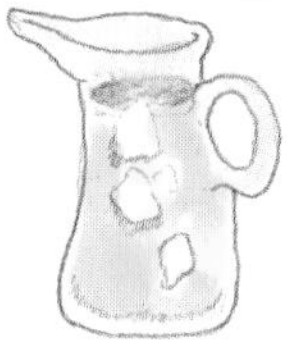 tea

Uu 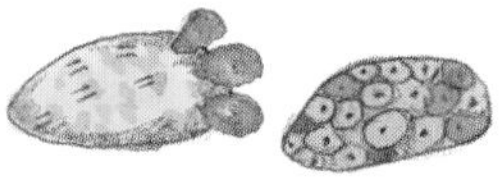 ugly fruit

Vv  vermicelli

Ww 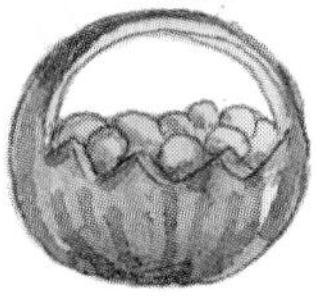 watermelon

Xx  extra jelly

Yy  yams

Zz 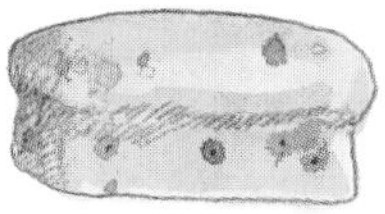 zucchini bread